Tink, North of
Never Land

This edition published by Parragon in 2012
Parragon
Queen Street House
4 Queen Street
Bath BA1 1HE, UK
www.parragon.com

ISBN 978-1-4454-7640-7

Printed in China

Tink, North of Never Land

Written by Kiki Thorpe
Illustrated by Judith Holmes Clarke,
Adrienne Brown & Charles Pickens

Bath • New York • Singapore • Hong Kong • Cologne • Delhi
Melbourne • Amsterdam • Johannesburg • Auckland • Shenzhen

"Last one to the meadow is a gooseberry!" Tinker Bell cried. "Terence, you don't stand a chance."

Tink took off flying. When the meadow came into view, she glanced back at her friend Terence, a fairy-dust-talent sparrow man. He was way behind.

Terence grinned. Suddenly he saw something hurtling through the air. It was headed right for Tink!

"Tink!" he yelled, "Look out!"

Tink looked up. She dodged out of the way just in time.

As the thing zoomed past, Tink realized it was Twire, a scrap-metal-recovery fairy. She struggled to hold a big metal object in her arms as she plummeted towards the ground.

"Twire!" Tink cried.

Twire let go of the metal object. It slammed to the ground. Twire crashed next to it, just missing a dairy mouse.

With a frightened squeak, the mouse took off running.

Tink and Terence rushed over to Twire. "Are you all right?" Terence asked.

Twire stood up. Her elbows and knees were scraped, and one of her wings was bent. But her glow was bright with excitement.

"Look what I found!" She pointed at the object. It was round and made of brass, with a glass front like that of a clock. But instead of two hands, it had a single, thin needle as long as a fairy's arm.

"What is it?" asked Terence.

Twire shook her head. "I don't

know. I found it on the beach. But just look at all that brass!"

Twire's talent was collecting bits of unwanted metal and melting them down so that they could be remade into useful things. Twire was always on the lookout for new types of metal to experiment with.

Terence nudged the object with his foot. "It's awfully heavy," he said. "Why didn't you use fairy dust to carry it?"

"I did. I guess I didn't use enough," Twire admitted.

"I've seen one of these before. It's called a compass," Tink said. "Compasses are very useful," she added.

Twire looked dismayed. If the

compass was still useful, she couldn't melt it down. "But this one's no good," she blurted out. "See how tarnished the brass is?"

"The brass doesn't matter. It's the needle that's important," Tink told her. "Whichever way you turn the compass, the needle should always point north."

Tink turned the compass to show them. She pushed the compass in a full circle. But instead of pointing north, the needle turned right along with the compass.

"It's broken!" Twire cried gleefully.

"I can fix it," Tink said.

Twire scowled at Tink. The two friends were often at odds. Tink always wanted to fix broken things while Twire wanted to melt them down.

Twire sighed. "All right, Tink, it's yours." She flew off to search for more metal.

Tink placed her hands on the compass. Her wings quivered with excitement. She had never fixed anything like it before.

"Want me to help you take the compass back to your workshop?" Terence asked. He liked Tink. He admired her talent for fixing things. There was no other fairy like her in all of Pixie Hollow.

Tink nodded.

Terence sprinkled the compass with fairy dust. Together, they lifted it into the air.

They reached Tink's workshop, carrying the compass between them. But when they tried to push the compass through the door, it got stuck.

"Now what?" asked Terence.

Tink thought for a moment. "I'll make it shrink," she said at last. The magic would be tricky, but Tink was sure she could do it.

She threw more fairy dust on the compass. Then she closed her eyes.

Terence is sweet, Tink thought. He would do anything to help a friend. He's also very talented. And his smile sparkles.

With a start, Tink realized that she wasn't thinking about the compass. She was thinking about Terence.

Tink opened her eyes. Terence smiled. "Can I help, Tink?" he asked.

Tink shook her head. She wished he weren't hovering so close. In fact, she suddenly wished he weren't there at all.

She closed her eyes again. This time, she thought only about the compass.

The compass began to shrink. As soon as Terence saw it change, he gave it a hard shove. The compass rolled into the room. It headed straight towards Tink's worktable. Terence darted forwards to stop it.

As he did, his wings swept a small

silver bowl off Tink's shelf.

The bowl spun across the floor, right into the path of –

"No!" Tink cried.

Crunch! The compass rolled over the bowl, crushing the metal.

Tink was shaking with anger.

Terence began to apologize. "I'd fly backwards – "

"Wherever I turn, you're under-wing," Tink yelled. "If you really wanted to help me, you'd leave me alone!"

Terence drew back. Without a word, he turned and flew away.

Tink watched Terence

leave. She frowned and tugged her bangs. Perhaps she'd spoken a little too harshly, and a little too quickly.

"But Terence *is* always in my way," she complained. "And now look what a mess he's made."

She examined the crumpled bowl. She ran her fingers lovingly over the silver. Tink adored anything made of metal. But this bowl was particularly special. It was the first thing she'd ever fixed as a pots-and-pans fairy.

Tink set to work fixing the bowl. Before long, she was lost in her work. She almost managed to forget all about Terence.

As Terence flew through Pixie Hollow, he hardly saw where he was going. He'd never known Tink felt that he was a bother.

"I'll leave Tink alone from now on," Terence vowed. The idea made him sad. But if she didn't want him around, he didn't want to be in her way.

Without noticing how he'd got there, Terence came to Minnow Lake.

Suddenly, something whipped by him in a blur. Terence looked up and saw the water fairy Silvermist gliding across the top of the lake on one foot.

Smiling, Silvermist skated up to

Terence. She noticed his gloomy expression right away.

"Why, Terence, you look as if you lost your best friend. I know what would cheer you up. Water-skating!" she said.

Terence watched as she twirled. "But only water talents can walk on water," he said.

"Wrong!" Silvermist replied. She spun on her toes and sped away.

Moments later, she returned with a pair of green sandals. She handed them to Terence.

"Put these skimmers on," Silvermist instructed. "They're made from lily-pads. They'll keep you afloat."

Terence strapped the lily-pad sandals on over his boots. He set one foot, then the other, down on the surface of the lake.

He was standing on water!

Terence took a careful step, then another. Then he took three giant steps, flapping his wings in between. Soon he was bounding around the lake.

For the first time since that morning, Terence smiled.

Tink stretched her arms high above her head and sighed happily. She had been working all afternoon. After she'd fixed the bowl, she had started on the compass.

"At this rate, I'll have it working again by tomorrow," she said with a smile.

Tink stood and flew out of her workshop, headed towards the orchard. She was feeling a little hungry. "I'll go and pick a cherry," she said.

As she passed Minnow Lake, Tink heard laughter.

That's Terence's laugh, she thought.

Suddenly, she remembered what had happened that morning. Maybe I was a little mean, thought Tink. She shrugged. Oh, well. She'd give him a friendly smile and show him that all was forgiven.

She flew to the lake. There was

Terence, skipping across the surface. Silvermist skated along beside him.

Tink waved at them from the shore. Silvermist didn't see her, but Terence did.

He was about to wave back. Then he remembered his vow. He turned and skated away.

Tink frowned. "Well," she said at last. "I'm glad Terence found someone to play with, at least."

And with a toss of her ponytail, she went on her way.

The next morning, Terence set off on his rounds. His job as a dust-talent was to make sure all the fairies and sparrow men of Pixie Hollow had enough dust to do their magic.

Terence tried not to think about Tinker Bell. But it wasn't easy. By the time he came upon the light-talent fairy Iridessa, Terence had been

24

unsuccessfully not-thinking about Tink for more than an hour.

Iridessa was headfirst in a large day-lily. The lily glowed from within like a giant orange lantern.

Terence gently tapped Iridessa's foot to let her know he was there.

Iridessa shrieked and popped her head up. "Terence! You could scare the fairy dust off someone!"

Terence sighed. "And it's my job to put the fairy dust *on* fairies." He scooped a cupful of dust from his sack and poured it over Iridessa. She shivered lightly as the dust settled on her.

"So, why are you collecting pollen?" Terence asked.

"Come on, I'll show you," Iridessa said.

She grabbed the basket of pollen and led Terence to a nearby clearing.

Holding up her hands, Iridessa began to pull sunlight out of the air. When she was done, she and Terence were sitting in a circle of darkness. It was the only spot in the clearing without daylight!

Then Iridessa took some of the sunlight and formed it into a bubble. She filled the bubble with pollen. Finally, she threw the bubble into the air as hard as she could.

Terence watched the bubble of light travel up, up, up. It burst with a pop, and golden pollen rained down. It looked just like fireworks.

"It's brilliant!" Terence said. Suddenly, he sprang to his feet. "I have an idea. Let's try using fairy dust."

Iridessa formed another ball of light. Terence filled it with dust.

The fairy-dust-filled bubble

floated out of Iridessa's hands even before she could throw it.

Just when Terence thought the bubble would drift out of the darkness and disappear, it exploded. The light shimmered with all of the bright colours of the rainbow.

Terence and Iridessa watched in awe.

"Got it!" Tink cried.

She stepped back and watched the compass needle swing around. As Tink turned the compass, the needle kept pointing north.

She sighed with pleasure and turned the compass a few more times, just to

admire her work.

Then she turned to show the compass to Terence.

She looked around her workshop.

Suddenly, Tink realized he wasn't there. Usually he stopped by to visit, but she hadn't seen him all day.

"I'll drop by the fairy-dust mill and see how he is," she said.

Tink flew to the mill and through the double doors. She saw several fairies and sparrow men at work. But Terence wasn't among them.

As she made her way back to the Home Tree, Tink saw a spark of light float up from a nearby field.

Tink flew over to take a look.

When she reached the field, she stopped and stared. In the centre was a small clearing. Though the sun shone brightly overhead, the clearing was as dark as night. Within the darkness, bursts of light bloomed like flowers.

Tink made out two tiny figures on the ground. One was her friend Iridessa. The other was Terence! With each new explosion, he and Iridessa clapped and cheered.

Tink hovered at the edge of the darkness, feeling left out.

That evening after dinner,
Tink hurried to the courtyard of the
Home Tree. It was time for the story-
talent fairies to spin their tales.

Tink looked around for Terence.
They usually sat together to listen to
the stories.

On the other side of the courtyard, Terence caught sight of Tink.
The seat next to him was empty, and

he wanted to call her over.

But we aren't friends anymore, he reminded himself.

Terence heard someone call his name. Rosetta, a garden fairy, was hovering behind him.

She pointed to the seat next to Terence. "Is someone sitting here?"

Terence shook his head.

Rosetta sat down. She carefully smoothed her rose-petal skirt and fluffed her hair. When she was finally settled, she turned to Terence. She smiled so brightly he couldn't help smiling back.

At that very moment, Tink finally spotted Terence. Her mouth fell open in surprise. He was sitting with Rosetta and they looked very happy to be together!

Tink felt a lump in the pit of her stomach. But before she could do anything, a hush settled over the crowd. The story was about to begin.

"*Pssst.* Tink!" Her friend Fawn, an animal-talent fairy, waved at her. "You can share with me."

Tink flew down and squeezed herself in next to Fawn.

The storyteller, Tor, stood in the centre of the courtyard. "Long, long ago, before the Home Tree, even before Mother Dove, there was the Pixie Dust Tree," he began.

Tink let out a small sigh. She knew the story of the Pixie Dust Tree well. It was one of her favourites.

"In those days, Pixie Hollow was a great land," Tor went on. "It covered mountains, forests and rivers."

As Tor spoke, the Pixie Dust Tree seemed to take shape before the fairies' eyes. Tink saw every detail, from its spiralling branches to its sturdy roots. That was the magic of story-talent fairies. Whatever they described became, in that moment, real.

The fairies saw Pixie Hollow as it once had been: purple mountains, crystal-clear streams, fields of sun-flowers stretching as far as the eye could see. And everywhere, fairies flying, playing and living happily.

Then, suddenly, the scene darkened. An evil force threatened the fairies' world. No storyteller would say its name out loud. It appeared as a black cloud, casting its shadow over Pixie Hollow.

The fairies in the story used every bit of magic they had, but in the end, they couldn't save everything. The dark cloud swallowed the Pixie Dust Tree.

"But in its place, the Home Tree grew," Tor told them. "It brought the Never fairies together. And we found Mother Dove, who gave us fairy dust again."

The fairies saw the image of Mother Dove. Her feathers shimmered.

"The Pixie Dust Tree is long gone," Tor told them, "But a bit of its dust still remains. It hangs in a cloud, just over the cliffs on the northern shore of Never Land. You can see it on certain nights."

A sparkling cloud seemed to hang in the air. As the fairies watched, it began to fade. Then it disappeared.

For a moment, the crowd was silent. Then one fairy sighed. The spell was broken. The story was over.

The crowd began to rise from their seats.

Tink heard Fawn's stomach growl. "Sad stories always make me hungry," Fawn explained. "Come with me to the tearoom?"

"Sure," said Tink. She glanced at Terence and added, "Maybe we should invite Terence and Rosetta too."

"Good idea," said Fawn. "Rosetta hates to miss dessert."

They flew towards Terence and Rosetta. But just as they reached them, the music fairies began to play a lively tune.

Rosetta sprang up from her seat. "This is my favourite song. Let's dance, Terence!"

She grabbed his hands and pulled him into the air. In the wink of an eye, the two had danced away.

Tink watched Terence

and Rosetta twirl through the air.
They didn't so much as glance in her
direction. She whirled around and
stormed off to her workshop.

Inside, she slammed the door
behind her. She kicked over a basket
of rivets.

"Every time I see Terence, he
ignores me!" she fumed. "And he

hasn't been by to visit since . . ."

Oh.

Tink sat down with a thump. Finally, it dawned on her: she'd told Terence to leave her alone.

I haven't been very nice to Terence, she thought and sighed. Her shoulders slumped.

But she wasn't one to mope for long. In Tink's opinion, problems were like broken pots. There wasn't one that couldn't be fixed.

"I'll win back his friendship!" she exclaimed. "I'll show everyone what a good friend I am."

She might have simply told him, "I'd fly backwards if I could." But she was too busy thinking of grander ways to show that she cared.

"I'll give him a present," she said. Her mind swirled with possibilities.

Terence is a dust-talent, she mused.

But he already had all the dust he could ever want.

Or did he? Tink remembered the end of Tor's story: "The Pixie Dust Tree is long gone. But a bit of its dust still remains."

That was it! She would bring Terence dust from the Pixie Dust Tree!

The Northern Shore was far from Pixie Hollow. It might take her days to get there. But the challenge only got Tink more excited.

"I'll leave tonight," she said.

Tink's eyes fell on the compass. Of course. It would point her right to the Northern Shore!

She began to pack, piling things on top of the compass – a sweater, a canteen, a sack of dried blueberries, a wool blanket, her spare dagger, a waterproof pouch to store her fairy dust in, some biscuits, a tin cup, a bag of tea . . .

Tink stepped back. The pile of things towered nearly to her chest. How in Never Land was she going to carry it all?

She snapped her fingers. "A balloon carrier!"

Balloon carriers were large fairy-dust-filled balloons with hanging baskets. She knew she shouldn't take one without telling anyone. But she

was afraid that if Queen Clarion heard of her plan, she would forbid Tink to go.

"I'll be gone for just a few days," she said. "I'm sure the others won't even miss it."

"I'll have to borrow it after everyone goes to bed," she whispered to herself.

So, drawing her little stool up to the window, Tink settled down to wait.

6

The moon was high in the sky when Tink loaded the balloon carrier. Then she picked up the carrier cord and rose into the air.

She continued up until she was above the tree line. Every few minutes, she looked at the compass. The needle pointed north, telling her exactly which way to go.

She'd been flying for a quarter

of an hour when she looked down.
Her heart sank. She was just crossing
Havendish Stream.

At this rate, it will take me weeks to
reach the Northern Shore! She thought.

But as luck would have it, the wind
shifted in Tink's direction.

In no time, she had reached the
edge of Pixie Hollow.

A moth flew up to the basket. It danced around Tink, drawn by her glow. She waved her arms, and the moth flew away.

Tink leaned back. High overhead, stars twinkled in the black sky. The basket gently rocked her and her eyelids grew heavy.

Within moments, Tink fell fast asleep.

Tink awoke with a start. The balloon had stopped moving.

She peeked over the side. The ropes that held the balloon to the basket were tangled in the branches of a large oak tree.

Tink climbed out of the basket and began to tug at the ropes.

Something snuffled behind her. She whirled around. A pair of red eyes stared at her from the darkness.

Tink gasped and sprang into the air. She could see more creatures in the branches around her. She was trapped!

One of the creatures began to move towards her. Tink flared her glow like a flame, hoping to scare it away.

It worked! The creature retreated to the other end of the branch. Tink saw the long, pointed nose of a possum. She knew that she was still

in trouble. Possums were bigger than she was, and she had accidentally dropped into their home.

Keeping an eye on the largest possum, Tink began to pull at the tangled ropes. Just as she grabbed the last rope, she heard a low growl. The possum bared her sharp teeth.

Tink gave a desperate tug, and the rope came free. She darted towards an opening in the branches, dragging the balloon after her. Then she flew out of the tree and kept on going.

Tink drifted in the balloon. She didn't care where the breeze took her, as long as it was away from the oak tree. When she checked the compass, she saw that she was still headed north.

A thin red glow appeared on the horizon, and Tink guided the carrier down to the edge of a small clearing. She tied the cord to a tree-root to anchor it, unrolled her blanket and curled up on a leaf. Finally, she slept.

7

When Tink opened her eyes,
she heard the sound of waves breaking
on a beach. That sound could mean
only one thing – she had reached the
Northern Shore!

Tink darted up into the air until
she could see over the tops of the trees.
Blue-green water shimmered in the
distance.

"The ocean!" cried Tink.

She raced back to her camp. Quickly, she ate a dried blueberry and washed it down with water from the canteen. Then she packed everything into the basket and took off through the forest.

The sound of the surf grew louder. Over the splash of the waves, she could hear a different noise, like a melody.

It sounds as if someone is singing, thought Tink.

When she emerged from the forest, Tink looked around. Soft white sand stretched a mile in every direction. Blue water gently lapped along the shore. Coconut palms rustled in the breeze.

This beach seems familiar, Tink thought.

She saw a large seaweed-covered rock rising from the water. A mermaid sat on top.

Tink's heart sank. She hadn't reached the Northern Shore at all. This was Mermaid Lagoon, less than an hour's flight from Pixie Hollow.

"But how?" Tink wailed. She had checked the compass over and over again.

Then she realized her mistake. Of course, a compass would be worthless on Never Land. For although a compass always pointed north, the island turned in whatever direction it wanted.

Tink threw the compass into the ocean. It vanished beneath the waves.

"I won't give up," she told herself. "I'll get to the Northern Shore if I have to fly for a week."

Tink stood and reached for the carrier cord. But it wasn't there. She spun around. The carrier was nowhere in sight.

Looking up, she spotted it high in the sky. She had forgotten to tie it down. As Tink watched, the carrier drifted over the top of a towering palm tree and was gone.

Tink clutched her head in horror.

She'd lost an entire balloon carrier!

But the carrier wasn't all she'd lost. Her food was gone, and so was her water. Luckily, she had kept her fairy dust with her.

Now she was more determined than ever to find the dust from the Pixie Dust Tree. She had to prove that her journey had been worthwhile.

She set off flying through the woods.

Tink flew all morning. When her shoulders ached too much to go on, she stopped beside a small spring and took a long drink of cool water. Then she sat down to rest.

She thought about the journey

ahead of her and shook her head. She had made so many mistakes. Maybe she had been wrong to come on this journey by herself.

Tink stood up and brushed away that thought. "I just need something to eat," she told herself.

Downstream, she spotted a gooseberry bush. She flew over to it.

Tink was trying to tug a berry from its stem, when she suddenly had the feeling she was being watched.

She dropped the berry and ducked into the bush. She scanned the forest. There was nothing –

No, wait! There! A pair of fox ears poked up from behind a hollow log.

Tink prepared to dart away.

The ears lifted. But they weren't attached to a fox. Beneath them was the face of a boy.

"Slightly!" Tink cried.

Slightly held his finger to his lips. But it was too late. There was a flash of green as something swooped down from above.

It was Peter Pan.

8

Tink grinned. She came out
of the bush and flew to meet Peter.

"Tink!" Peter exclaimed. "You're
just in time. I was about to find
Slightly." Peter reached over and
tapped Slightly on the head. "And
now you're *it*."

At the word "it" there was a rustle
in the bushes. Cubby, Nibs and the
Twins emerged out from their hiding

places.

Tink looked at the boys. Someone was missing.

"Where's Tootles?" she asked Peter.

Peter shrugged. "Sometimes he falls asleep. Tootles! Tootles, come out!" he called.

Suddenly, one of the Twins cried out. "Peter, look! Tootles's footprints go to here. Then they disappear!"

Peter leapt down to study the tracks. "Disappeared right into thin air. There's only one thing that could have happened. . . . Tootles has been *kidnapped!*"

Tink gasped.

Peter turned to the Lost Boys.

"Men, we must rescue Tootles."

Swept up in the excitement, Tink forgot all about her search for the pixie dust. They set off marching through the forest.

They hadn't gone far, though, when Tink cried out, "Look!" She landed next to a paw-print in the mud.

"Tracks! Good job, Tink," Peter said. "The print belongs to a tiger. A big one, from the look of it!"

Tink, Peter and the boys followed the tracks. They circled right back to the place where Tootles's tracks ended.

Peter shook his head sadly. "Poor Tootles has been eaten by a tiger."

All the boys stared at Peter.

"Bow your heads, fellas," Peter instructed. "Poor old Tootles."

Sniffing loudly, the Lost Boys lowered their heads. Tink landed on Peter's shoulder and solemnly dimmed her glow.

Rrrrow! Suddenly, they heard a

loud growl above them.

"The tiger!" Cubby shrieked.

Tink flew up into the tree branches. She began to laugh. "That's no tiger," she said. "It's Tootles!"

Tootles looked down from the rope that held him. "I think I found the best hiding spot," he said.

A few days before, Peter and the Lost Boys had rigged the trap, hoping to catch a tiger. Tootles had stumbled into it by mistake when he was looking for a hiding place.

Peter flew up to the tree branch. He drew his knife to cut down the rope. As he did, they heard a low, deep growl. All heads swivelled to look at Tootles.

"Wasn't me," Tootles said with a shrug.

"The tiger!" Peter cried, just as a huge beast sprang from the bushes.

Up in the air, Tootles, Peter and Tink were safe. But the tiger was headed straight for the other Lost Boys.

Without thinking, Tink turned her sack of fairy dust upside down over them. "Fly!" she yelled.

The Lost Boys leapt into the air.

On the ground, the tiger prowled. It twitched its tail and watched them with yellow eyes.

"Can't catch us!" Peter cried at the tiger.

Finally, the tiger slunk away. When they were sure it was gone, Peter cut Tootles down.

"If it wasn't for Tink, you'd have been his dinner," Peter told the boys.

"Hooray for Tinker Bell!" they cheered. Tink's glow turned pink as she blushed.

"She should get an award for bravery," Peter said. He pulled a golden bead out of his pocket and threaded a piece of grass through it. Then he hung it around Tink's neck.

"We present this medal to Tinker Bell," he announced, "the best and bravest fairy in Never Land."

Tink's heart swelled. Why had she

ever doubted herself? She checked the bag of fairy dust. There was still a little left in the bottom.

"Peter, I have to fly to the Northern Shore," she said. "I'll see you again soon." Then, clutching her medal to her chest, she set out once again.

By sunset, Tink felt sure she was close to the Northern Shore. She flew over a crest. Ahead, the ground dropped away into ocean. Waves pounded the rocks on the shore.

The Northern Shore! Tink marvelled. I made it!

There could be no doubt about it this time. A glowing silver cloud hovered in the air. It's the cloud of pixie dust, Tink thought.

Within moments, she was skimming over the water. The sound of the surf roared in her ears. Spray from the crashing waves soaked her from head to toe.

But where was the pixie dust?

Tink found a dry nook high up on the side of a rock. From her spot, she once again looked for the pixie dust. There it was!

The sky had darkened and just then, a cloud passed over the moon. Before Tink's eyes, the pixie dust changed.

"It's nothing but mist!" Tink's voice trembled. What she had

thought was a cloud of pixie dust was
only spray from the surf.

"I came all this way for nothing,"
she said. "I . . . I failed."

She ripped the medal Peter had

given her from her neck. "Best," she sneered. "I'm not the best at anything."

She opened her hand and let it fall. The bead bounced off the side of the rock and sank into the ocean.

Tink flew slowly back through the forest towards Pixie Hollow.

After all her efforts, she had nothing to give Terence. "He will never want to be my friend now," Tink murmured.

Suddenly, Tink heard a crashing sound not far away.

Someone groaned. "Oh, no."

Tink darted through a tangle of

vines. She spotted a big hole in the ground. She crept to the edge and peeped in.

There was Tootles, staring back at her.

"Tink!" he cried happily.

"What are you doing down there?" asked Tink.

"Oh." Tootles blushed. "I fell into another trap. We dug this one to catch a bear. Can you give me some fairy dust so I can fly out?"

Tink only had the fairy dust left on her wings. There wasn't enough to help Tootles fly out of the hole.

She spotted a long, thick vine hanging from a nearby tree. She

pulled the end of the vine close to the hole and threw it over the edge.

Tootles grabbed it, and he pulled himself out. "Promise not to tell Peter?" he asked.

Tink nodded.

"Tinker Bell, you should have an award for bravery," he said, trying to sound like Peter.

He pulled a sparrow feather from his cap. Solemnly, Tootles held out the feather to Tink.

Tink turned it over in her hands.

"It's the best thing I've got," Tootles said. "I hope you'll take good care of it." With a wave, he ran off to find the other boys.

Tink stood for a moment, looking at the feather. Then she leapt up and began to fly towards home. She knew what she had to do.

Tink got back to Pixie Hollow just before dinner time. As she neared the Home Tree kitchen, she smelled chestnuts roasting. Her mouth watered. For two days, she'd had nothing to eat but berries.

But there was something she had to do before she could eat.

When she reached her workshop, Tink stopped short in surprise.

Terence, Silvermist, Iridessa, Rosetta and Fawn were standing outside her door.

Tink hovered uncertainly. What are they doing here? she wondered.

They were waiting for her!

Terence had been the first to notice she was missing when she didn't show up to breakfast days ago. After searching all over Pixie Hollow, they had gone to her workshop to wait. And to worry.

Silvermist, Iridessa, Rosetta and Fawn rushed over to her.

"Tink, where have you been?" cried Silvermist.

"We were so worried!" Rosetta added.

"What happened to you?" asked Fawn.

As Tink's friends surrounded her,

Terence hung back. He wasn't sure she would be glad to see him.

"Tink, what you need is a hot bath," said Silvermist. "I'll bring you some warm water."

"You need something to eat," said Iridessa. "How does sunflower soup sound?"

"You'll feel much better in a clean dress," said Rosetta. "And I have the perfect thing! I'll be back before you can say 'gorgeous'."

"You need a nap!" said Fawn. "You can borrow my fluffy feather pillow."

The four fairies flew off. Terence started to follow them.

"Terence, wait," Tink said.

She couldn't give him dust from the Pixie Dust Tree. But she could give him something else. And now Tink understood that the gift wasn't important. What mattered was how it was given.

She went to the shelf in her workshop and took down the silver bowl. She placed it in Terence's hands.

"It's a perfect repair," he said. "You can't even tell it was bent. You're the best pots-and-pans fairy around, Tink." He started to hand it back.

But Tink shook her head. "It's for you."

"Why?" Terence asked, startled.

"For being my friend," said Tink.

"But . . . I've been trying *not* to be your friend. You told me to leave you alone."

Now Tink laughed. "I didn't mean for *good!*" she exclaimed. "I was upset. But I'm not anymore. I've been all over

Never Land looking for the perfect present for you." She pointed to the bowl. "It was my first fix ever. I hope you'll take good care of it."

Finally, Terence understood. The bowl might have looked like just a silver bowl, but coming from Tink, it was much more than that. It was an apology.

He smiled. "I know just the place for it."

Then, to Tink's surprise, he flew over and placed it back on her shelf. He didn't need the bowl. Tink's friendship was all he'd ever wanted.

"I think it will be safe here," he told Tink. "And I can come by to visit it. Now, shall we go to dinner?"

Tink laughed. She was messy and covered in dirt, but it didn't matter. She took Terence's hand. Together, the two friends flew out into the evening.

Join the Disney Fairies on their next Pixie Hollow adventure...

Silvermist and the Ladybird Curse

Sunlight sparkled on the cool, clear waters of Havendish Stream. Silvermist, a water-talent fairy, waded in and took the oak-leaf cover off her tiny birch-bark canoe.

The fairies and sparrow men of Pixie Hollow were getting ready for a special picnic on an island not far from the shore.

Silvermist smiled as she stepped out
of the water. "This picnic will be the
best ever," she told Dulcie, a
baking-talent.

Dulcie nodded. She held out a picnic
basket for Silvermist to take. "Here are
some muffins and berry juice."

"I'll help!" said Silvermist's friend Fira, a light-talent fairy. She reached for the basket and put it in the canoe.

Rani, another water-talent, pushed off in another canoe. She began to paddle towards the island.

One by one, the rest of the water fairies followed. Other talents hovered above the canoes, trailing the boats towards the island.

"Are you coming, Silvermist?" Fira asked.

"I promised Iris I would take something for her," Silvermist replied. "I'll catch up!"

"Okay, but hurry," Fira said. "It's

almost high noon. The perfect time for a picnic."

Silvermist watched Fira join the others. Then she settled back and took in the scene. It all looked so lovely. The canoes drifted in rows, while the fairies flew gracefully above.

"Silvermist! Silvermist! I'm here!" Iris called out. The garden-talent fairy rushed up with an armful of messy-looking wildflowers. She placed them in the canoe. "Whew! I knew you wouldn't leave before I got here!"

Silvermist glanced at the flowers. "What are they?"

"They are very rare chrysanthe-poppies. I searched every field in Pixie Hollow just to find them."

Silvermist examined the flowers. They looked more like weeds than anything else. But taking them to the picnic obviously meant a lot to Iris, so Silvermist was happy to help her.

"I'm going now!" Iris said as she flew away. "Don't bump the canoe too much, Silvermist. The flowers are very delicate!"

Silvermist paddled away from the shore. Most of the other fairies were already on the island, but the day was so beautiful, Silvermist decided to take her time and enjoy the trip.

"Moving a bit slowly today, sweetheart?" asked Vidia, a fast-flying fairy, as she landed lightly on the end of Silvermist's canoe.

"Are you going to the picnic?" Silvermist asked. Vidia didn't usually attend fairy gatherings.

Vidia laughed. "Goodness, no. I just happened to be flying by, and I saw all these fairies happily picnicking on the island. You however, sweetie, seem to have 'missed the boat,' so to speak, going at a snail's pace."

Silvermist just shrugged. She was nearing the island. Fira waved to her from the shore.

Vidia frowned. Usually she could get a rise out of the other fairies. But her words had no effect on Silvermist.

"How are my flowers doing?" Iris shouted to Silvermist from the water's edge.

"Flowers? Is that what those weeds are?" Vidia leaned over to take a closer look.

The canoe tipped.

"Oh!" Vidia cried as her feet slipped out from under her. With a loud splash, she fell into the water.

Other titles in this series:

Beck and the
Great Berry Battle

Fawn and the Mysterious
Trickster

Iridessa, Lost at Sea

Lily's Pesky Plant

Silvermist and the
Ladybird Curse

The Trouble with Tink

Vidia and the Fairy Crown